D1604742

Mr. Bear's Chair

THOMAS GRAHAM

E. P. Dutton • New York

Copyright © 1987 by Thomas Graham
All rights reserved.

Library of Congress Cataloging in Publication Data
Graham, Thomas, date
  Mr. Bear's chair.
  Summary: When Mrs. Bear's chair breaks, Mr. Bear
spends all day making her a new one that's just right.
  [1. Bears—Fiction.   2. Chairs—Fiction]   I. Title.
PZ7.G7579Mr 1987   [E]   86-19920
ISBN 0-525-44300-2

Published in the United States by E. P. Dutton,
2 Park Avenue, New York, N.Y. 10016

Published simultaneously in Canada by
Fitzhenry & Whiteside Limited, Toronto

Designer: Isabel Warren-Lynch

Printed in Hong Kong by South China Printing Co.
First Edition   COBE   10 9 8 7 6 5 4 3 2 1

3 1172 02094 5333

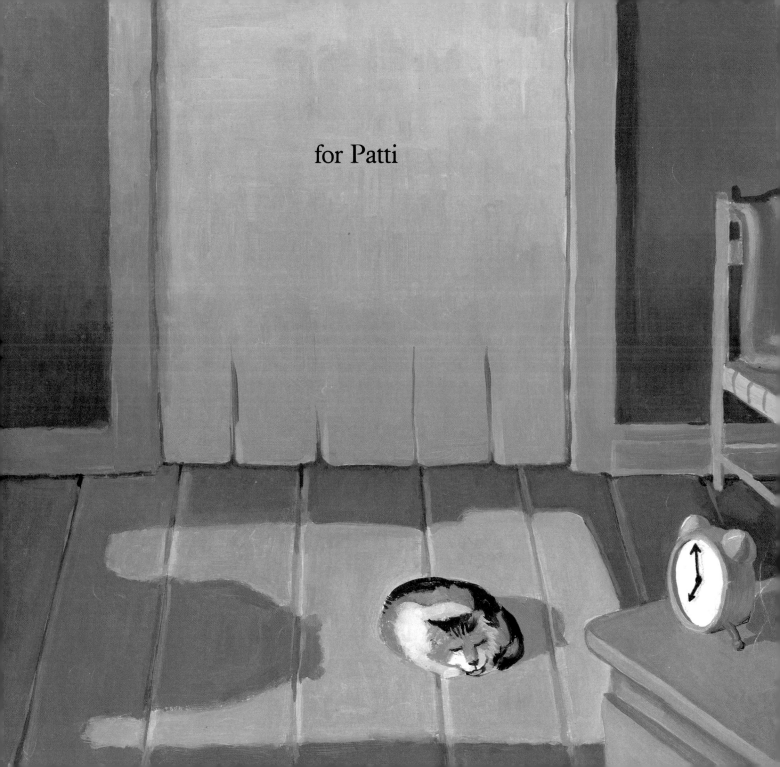

for Patti

"Breakfast is ready," called Mr. Bear.
Mr. Bear loved to make pancakes, and Mrs. Bear loved to eat them.

But when Mrs. Bear sat down…*CRASH!*

Mrs. Bear was very cross.
"Just you wait," said Mr. Bear. "I'll have a
surprise for you by supper."

Mr. Bear headed for an old hickory tree.

He knew exactly what to do. He swung
his axe, hard.

He sawed the tree trunk to just
the right lengths.

He split the lengths to just the right thicknesses.

Then he shaved

and planed

and drilled

and chiseled.

He counted and thought.

He knew by the sound when the parts fit just right.

And they all did.

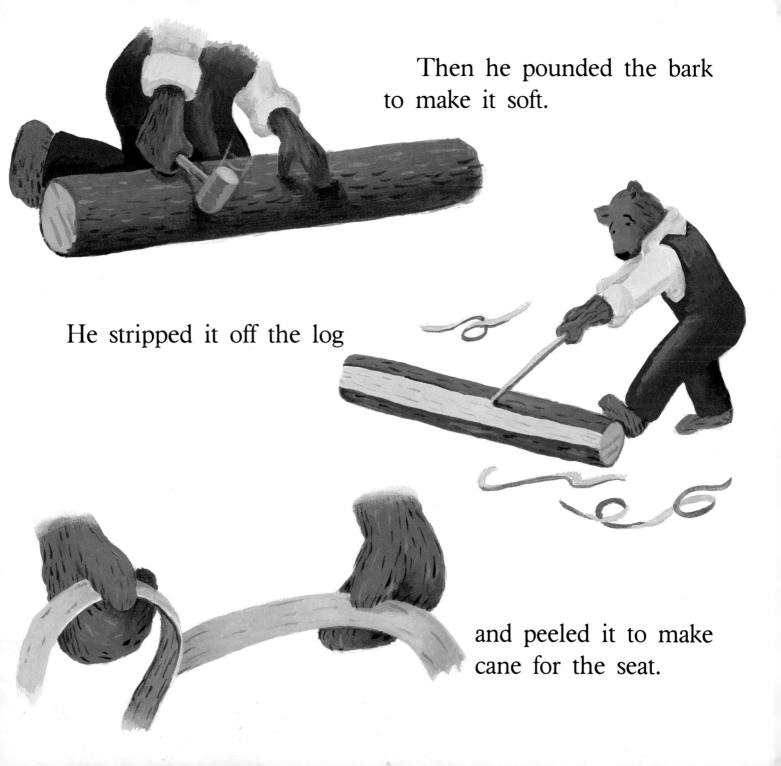

Then he pounded the bark
to make it soft.

He stripped it off the log

and peeled it to make
cane for the seat.

Mr. Bear carefully wove the cane, under and over, under and over.

He hoped Mrs. Bear would like the chair.

She did.

Mrs. Bear put supper on the table.
"Turkey!" said Mr. Bear. "My favorite!"
He sat down. And...

CRASH!